NO! NO! NO!

E
ROC

by Anne Rockwell

Macmillan Books for Young Readers • New York

Today was going to be a terrible day.
I knew it would be,
the minute I got out of bed.

"No, no, no!" I said
at breakfast.
"I don't like cereal with holes!"
I didn't like my orange juice, either.
So I didn't care
when it spilled all over the kitchen floor.

The toothpaste tasted awful

and I had to wear that yucky plaid shirt.

"No, no, no!" I said.
"I don't want to wear my raincoat!"

But I had to.

At school, the picture I made was awful

and all my blocks fell down.

I forgot to bring my show-and-tell,
and Sarah said my new shoes
were funny looking.

On my way home, I fell in the mud.

Then I couldn't find
my brand-new, super-shiny purple car.

My soup was too hot
and my pudding wasn't chocolate.

The sliced apple tasted all right,
but our dog ate most of it.

"No, no, no! I don't want
to take a bath!" I said.
But I had to, just the same.
Yuck!
I didn't like the way
those bubbles smelled,
and when I got out of the tub,
my new pajamas felt all itchy.

"I don't like it!" I said
when the wrong cartoon came on.
"Okay," my mother said.
"I can see it's time for bed."

"No! No! No!" I yelled,
but it didn't do any good.
I tell you—there was nothing at all,
not one single thing that went right today.

But guess what?
Soon everything began to change.
My mother read me a brand new book—
the very best book in all the world.
And when I fell asleep,
I had a beautiful dream!

So, when I woke up next morning,
it was the start of today!

For Nigel John

Copyright © 1995 by Anne Rockwell
Macmillan Books for Young Readers
An imprint of Simon & Schuster Children's Publishing Division
Simon & Schuster Macmillan
1230 Avenue of the Americas
New York, New York 10020

All rights reserved including the right of reproduction in whole or in part in any form.
Designed by Cathy Bobak.
The text of this book is set in 19 point ITC Cheltenham Book.
Printed and bound in Hong Kong on recycled paper.
First edition
10 9 8 7 6 5 4 3 2 1
Library of Congress Cataloging-in-Publication Data
Rockwell, Anne F.
No! No! No! / by Anne Rockwell.
p.   cm.
Summary: After a day when nothing goes right, a young boy's mood
begins to change at bedtime.
ISBN 0-02-777782-0
[1. Mood (Psychology)—Fiction.]   I. Title.
PZ7.R5943Nr   1995
[E]—dc20   94-26190